For my beloved Oskar.
Britta

LITTLE TIGER KIDS

An imprint of the Little Tiger Group

1 Coda Studios, 189 Munster Road, London SW6 6AW • www.littletiger.co.uk

First published in Great Britain 2017 • Text by Patricia Hegarty • Text copyright © 2017 Little Tiger Press Ltd.

Illustrations copyright © Britta Teckentrup 2017 • A CIP Catalogue record for this book is available from the British Library

MOON

Illustrated by
Britta Teckentrup

Have you ever wondered why
The moon shines in the night-time sky?

How every creature, plant and tree
Is subject to its mystery...

A breeze blows softly across the land,
Rippling through the grass and sand.

A scorpion scuttles through the night,
Glowing with an eerie light.

Far away, in a land harsh and bare,
Puffins shiver in the cold night air.

The Northern lights set the skies aglow,
Shimmering, glimmering, above the snow.

As birds fly south to warmer climes
They seem to sense the perfect time.

Journeying on all through the night,
The moon will always guide their flight.

In the jungle, through a canopy of green,
Shafts of silvery light can be seen.

As parrots swoop beneath the moon,
Tree frogs chirrup their nightly tune.

On southern shores, on a moonlit night,
Nature reveals a magical sight.

Hundreds of turtles swim to land,
To lay their eggs in soft white sand.

When nights are dark and the moon is new,
A tiny field mouse has work to do.

Busily scampering here and there,
He hunts for food in the cool night air.

The ocean sparkles, bluey-green,
Lit up by a magical scene.

Waves roll gently to and fro...
The moon commands their ebb and flow.

Above the mountainside at night,
The sky is filled with sparkling light.

As wispy clouds scutter by,
A shining moonbow lights the sky.

In the grassland all is still,
Animals rest in the night-time chill.

After the day's blistering heat,
The cool clear air smells fresh and sweet.

Snowflakes fall on frozen ground,
Swirling, twirling, they make no sound.

Under the moon, huddled together,
Penguins seek warmth in the icy weather.

So, when you close your eyes at night,
The moon reflects the sun's soft light,

Shining down with a silvery glow,
As we dream our dreams in the world below.